D0922308

Let That Bad Air Out
plays like New Orleans jazz itself.
From intro and ensemble, it
builds through the wildest of solos
to the inevitable, all-spending
climax. The images are silent, but
you can hear the music in every
one.

Patrick Tevlin, bandleader,
the Happy Pals New Orleans
Party Orchestra

For the Happy Pals New Orleans Party Orchestra,
with special thanks to Justin Lebine and George Walker

Dec 18/08

Allan.
Thanks for sharing
your talent to
commemorate this
special day!.
Canada Council
of UNESCO.

LET THAT BAD AIR OUT

BUDDY BOLDEN'S LAST PARADE

STEFAN BERG

The Porcupine's Quill

Library and Archives Canada Cataloguing in Publication

Berg, Stefan, 1985 –

Let that bad air out : Buddy Bolden's last parade / by Stefan Berg.

ISBN 978-0-88984-296-0

1. Berg, Stefan, 1985 –.   2. Bolden, Buddy, ca. 1868–1931 –
Pictorial works.   3. Artists' books – Canada.   I. Title.

NE543.B47A4 2007   769.92   C2007-904137-X

Published by The Porcupine's Quill, 68 Main St, Erin,
Ontario NOB 1TO. http://www.sentex.net/˜pql

Readied for the press by George Walker, with Tim Inkster
and Terri Janovich.

Represented in Canada by the Literary Press Group.
Trade orders are available from University of Toronto Press.

We acknowledge the support of the Ontario Arts Council and the
Canada Council for the Arts for our publishing program. The financial
support of the Government of Canada through the Book Publishing
Industry Development Program is also gratefully acknowledged.
Thanks, also, to the Government of Ontario through the Ontario
Media Development Corporation's Ontario Book Initiative.

ONTARIO ARTS COUNCIL
CONSEIL DES ARTS DE L'ONTARIO

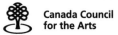

Canada Council   Conseil des Arts
for the Arts   du Canada

PREFACE

I was first introduced to the sound of New Orleans jazz at Grossman's Tavern on Spadina in downtown Toronto, by a band called the Happy Pals. Michael Ondaatje's novel, *Coming Through Slaughter*, furthered my interest in the legend of Buddy Bolden in particular. I imagined creating a silent novel about a particular kind of music and expressing the energy of a New Orleans parade through the medium of still images. Film footage from the late 1950s, of the Eureka Brass Band marching on Claiborne Avenue, gave me a sense of how my story would look on the page.

The drawing process was absolutely essential in developing the structure behind the linocut block images. Drawings were overlaid, redrawn continually and combined with collaged photography. This methodology enabled a rich quality of depth and a full spectrum of space. Cutting into the blocks was, in itself, a second editing process. I was able to reevaluate the images even as they were being finalized. I had chosen linoleum as a cutting surface for this reason. The original proofs were then hand-printed by Justin Labine and myself, in black ink on a Grafix Proofing Press.

In pursuing this project I find I have embraced the express-ionists completely – the sensation of raw emotion, of exposed nerves and explosive actions. These are all qualities inherent in the relief print. What translates from the block to paper is something of the spontaneity of linocutting, juxtaposed with strategic, highly constructed marks of precision.

Stefan Berg, August 2007

INTRODUCTION

Charles Joseph 'Buddy' Bolden was born in New Orleans on
September 6, 1877. Buddy Bolden's father, Westmore, most
certainly would have taken his young son to watch and absorb
the sounds of the New Orleans parades. Buddy began to play
the cornet at an early age and by 1895 was already the leader of
his own group. He had acquired a reputation by the turn of the
century and a few years later was widely acknowledged to be
the 'hottest' musician in the city.

His career was tragically short. It was at a Labour Day parade
in 1906 that Buddy Bolden played his last notes before
collapsing on the street and being remanded for insanity.
Before his thirtieth birthday he was committed to the asylum
in Jackson, Louisiana. He never left, and died there in 1931.

Whether Buddy Bolden can truly be said to have 'invented' jazz
has always been the subject of much speculation and
controversy. My personal feeling is that no one man invented
jazz, and no specific date of origin can be fixed. Brass bands
have been a tradition in New Orleans since its very beginning.
Every ethnic group took pride in the quality of their martial
music. As the bands marched on the streets, the entire
populace would come out to listen. The parades were long,
stretching out for many miles and continuing for hours. After
the parades there would be a concert, and later still a dance. A
fifteen-hour day was not unusual. These musical celebrations
were staged on Labour Day, Mardi Gras, other holidays, and at
political events. In the black community a funeral with brass
band music was, as Jelly Roll Morton once said, 'the end of a
perfect death'.

Buddy Bolden was a legendary figure in the New Orleans music scene, but no one knew much about him. Some older musicians such as Jelly Roll Morton, Sidney Bechet and Kid Ory deferred to Bolden as 'the man who started it all'. But there was no accurate documentation, and, of course, his music had never been recorded.

I became interested in Buddy Bolden in the mid-1960s. At the time, I held a position at the New Orleans Public Library, which had recently acquired a wealth of documentary material pertaining to the city's history, including birth, marriage and death certificates. These records had not previously been available to the public, and they opened up to me an entirely new way to research early New Orleans music and musicians. The certificates not only proved that there really was a Buddy Bolden, they also supplied many new details about his family, his personal history and the places where he had lived.

Today Bolden is considered, along with Jelly Roll, King Oliver, Bechet, Louis Armstrong and many others, to be an integral part of New Orleans' music (or jazz) history.

I am impressed with Stefan Berg's atention to critical detail, such as the band, the buildings and the atmosphere. *Let That Bad Air Out* is a great addition to the Bolden story.

Donald M. Marquis
Author of *In Search Of Buddy Bolden:*
First Man Of Jazz,
winner of the Louisiana Literary award for 1978

21

III

123

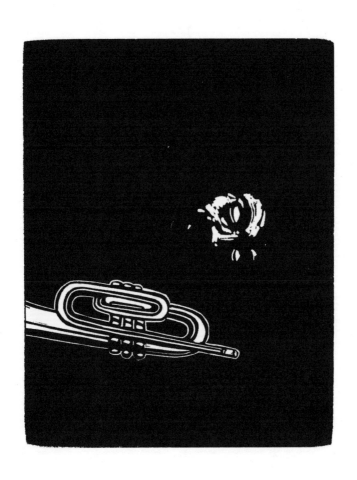

AFTERWORD

Wordless novels first appeared after the First World War when the Flemish artist Frans Masereel applied his creative genius to the making of books 'written' in wood engravings, telling a story without the use of the printed word. Masereel's books, beginning with *The Passion of a Man* (1918), marked the dawn of the sequential picture narrative that would reach its zenith in the 1930s with the work of the American Lynd Ward (*God's Man, Vertigo, Madman's Drum, Wild Pilgrimage*) and fall into obscurity in the 1950s when the last wood engraved wordless novel (*Southern Cross*, 1951) appeared, written by the Canadian Laurence Hyde. Stories told in pictures have a universality that transcends the boundaries of any spoken or written language, providing the reader with a unique experience of narrative not unlike that of the silent film.

Let That Bad Air Out is the first in a projected series of wordless novels to be published by the Porcupine's Quill. The aim of this project is to publish wordless books created using the relief printmaking techniques of linocut, woodcut or wood engraving. Each title in the series will feature original work created by contemporary printmakers. The reason for choosing relief printmaking to illustrate these stories is not only to pay homage to the artists who started the tradition of the wordless novel but also to help revive interest and appreciation of the rich qualities of line and texture available with relief printmaking. This style of printmaking is not dead and forgotten, but is alive and blossoming in the youthful hands of artists such as Stefan Berg. Stefan Berg's story of the great jazz cornet player Buddy Bolden is a fine narrative for a story in linocuts. Berg (a former student of mine) is obsessed with the story of Bolden whose tragic death and legendary playing have awed jazz historians for decades. Berg takes us through a New Orleans parade where we find Bolden standing out from the band, captivating his audience before falling victim to a mental breakdown. Although no recordings of this legendary jazz musician can be found, we can again appreciate Bolden's influence, quietly, with Berg's story in pictures.

George A. Walker

ABOUT THE ARTIST

Stefan Berg is a painter and printmaker who was born at Toronto in 1985. He is currently (2007) completing his final year at the Ontario College of Art and Design. An up-coming artist on the Toronto art scene, Stefan curated the 2005 Collage Methodologies group show, and participates in several independent print collectives including the End Street Studio and the Free North Press. Stefan currently works with intaglio and relief printmaking mediums. He has been featured in the Canadian small press publications 'Cut And Print' and 'Block Cutters Social Klub', published by the Free North Press. The Free North Press has also published Stefan's first independent book *After a while*, a selection of block work 2002–2006.

The recipient of multiple scholarships for excellence in painting, photography and printmaking, including a post graduate entry scholarship, Stefan's intent is to uphold the traditional methods of printmaking as a contemporary artist.

A selection of his artwork is included in the Grossmans' collection, Toronto, as well as in several other private Canadian collections.